# WOMAN'S JOURNAL
## AND SUFFRAGE NEWS

VOL. XLIV. NO. 10 SATURDAY, MARCH 8, 1913 FIVE CENTS

## PARADE STRUGGLES TO VICTORY DESPITE DISGRACEFUL SCENES

### Nation Aroused by Open Insults to Women—Cause Wins Popular Sympathy—Congress Orders Investigation—Striking Object Lesson

Washington has been disgraced. Equal suffrage has scored a great victory. Thousands of indifferent women have been aroused. Influential men are incensed and the United States Senate demands an investigation of the treatment given the suffragists at the National Capital on Monday.

Ten thousand women from all over the country had planned a magnificent parade and pageant to take place in Washington on March 3. Artists, pageant leaders, designers, women of influence and renown were ready to give a wonderful and beautiful piece of suffrage work to the public that would throng the National Capital for the inauguration festivities. The suffragists were ready; the whole procession started down Pennsylvania avenue, when the police protection, that had been promised, failed them, and a disgraceful scene followed. The crowd surged into the space which had been marked off for the paraders, and the leaders of the suffrage movement were compelled to push their way through a mob of the worst element in Washington and vicinity. Women were spit upon, slapped in the face, tripped up, pelted with burning cigar stubs, and insulted by jeers and obscene language too vile to print or repeat.

The cause of all the trouble is apparent when the facts are known. The police authorities in Washington opposed every attempt to have a suffrage parade at all. Having been forbidden a place in the inaugural procession, the suffragists asked to have a procession of their own on March 3. They were finally told that they could have a procession but that it could not be on Pennsylvania avenue, but must be on a side street. At last they got permission to have the suffrage parade on the avenue, and asked that traffic be excluded from the street during the parade. For a long time this was denied, and only on Saturday were they successful.

Everything was at last arranged; it was a glorious day; ten thousand women were ready to do their part to make the parade beautiful to behold, to make it a credit to womanhood and to demonstrate the strength of the movement for their enfranchisement.

The police were determined, however, and they had their way. Their attempt to afford the marchers protection and keep the space of the avenue free for the suffrage procession was the flimsiest sham. Police officers stood by with folded arms and grinned while the picked women of the land were insulted and roughly abused by an ignorant and uncouth mob.

Miss Alice Paul and other suffragists were compelled to drive their automobiles down the avenue to separate the crowds so the suffragists with the banners and floats could pass. The police officials say their force was inadequate to handle the crowds, but it is noted that there was no disorder on the avenue during the inaugural procession. It is stated that federal troops were offered to the chief of police for the suffrage procession, but that he refused their aid.

At any rate, assistance was finally called from Fort Myer and mounted soldiers drove back the crowd so that a straggling line of marchers could pass through.

Not only were the suffragists bit[terly] disappo[inted] ...

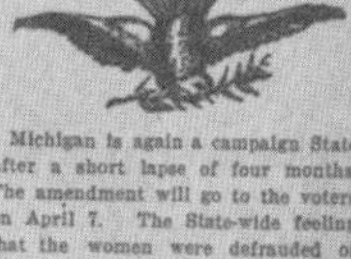

...s of Imposing Floats;

## AMENDMENT WINS IN NEW JERSEY

### Easy Victory in Assembly 46 to 5—Equal Suffrage Enthusiasm Runs High

The New Jersey Legislature passed the woman suffrage amendment in the Assembly last week by a vote of 46 to 5. The Senate had already voted favorably 14 to 5.

A large delegation of suffragists crowded the galleries, and when the overwhelming vote was announced there was a scene of great enthusiasm. Women stood in their seats and waved handkerchiefs and "votes for women" flags and cheered themselves hoarse.

**Dr. Jekyll Becomes Mr. Hyde**

Opposition was confined exclusively to the old sentimental arguments.

(Continued on Page 79)

## MICHIGAN AGAIN CAMPAIGN STATE

### Senate Passes Suffrage Amendment 26 to 5 and Battle Is Now On

Michigan is again a campaign State after a short lapse of four months. The amendment will go to the voters on April 7. The State-wide feeling that the women were defrauded of victory last fall will help the suffragists.

The final action of the Legislature was taken last week, when the Senate, by a vote of 26 to 5, passed the suffrage amendment, with a slight amendment to make the requirements for foreign-born women the same as those for male immigrants.

**Governor Watches Debate**

The debate in the Senate lasted an hour and a quarter, and was characterized by the persistent efforts of Senator Weadock and a few others to tack on crippling amendments. Several suggestions, including the disabling of women for holding office or serving on juries, were voted down in quick succession.

Gov. Ferris was among the visitors who crowded the chamber and gallery. Mrs. Clara B. Arthur, Mrs. Thomas R. Henderson and Mrs. Wilbur Brotherton, of Detroit; Mrs. Jennie Law Hardy, of Tecumseh, and other State leaders were present, supported by a large delegation of Lansing suffragists.

The final stand of the opposition was made by Senator Murtha in the hope of putting off the submission till November, 1914, and this also failed.

Of the five who opposed the measure on the final roll-call, three were from Detroit.

A complete campaign of organization and education has been mapped out by the State Association. The

(Continued on Page 74.)

SAN FRANCISCO CHRONICLE

SUND...



## Vete... ...kes De... ...igh California Mountain Tops

Chronicle

### Seventieth Anniversary of Birth Celebrated With Typical Ceremony

Nov 14, 1926

Rear-Admiral Charles Fremont Pond, retired naval officer and one of Berkeley's most noted disciples of the out-of-doors, celebrated his seventieth birthday recently in a manner said by his friends to be characteristic.

Instead of surrounding himself with companions of his many years on the high seas, the navy man observed the seventh decade of his eventful life with intimate friends connected with the activity he has championed since his retirement—hiking.

Each year since 1918, when he left off active participation in naval affairs and settled down in the Berkeley residence he had maintained for many years before, Admiral Pond has led summer parties of friends on strenuous tramps into the high Sierra. Many of these excursions included outstanding figures in University of California circles, among whom were Prof. Joseph LeConte, Willard Grinnell, son of the ornithologist; Miss Mary Elizabeth Plehn, Mary Isabel Wocker, George Stewart McManus, Joseph and Helen LeConte and Ansel E. Adams.

Last summer the Admiral and his daughter, Elizabeth, were leaders in the tramp during the month of June which took them into some of the most remote and inaccessible spots of the mountainous region of Five Lake basin, Cloudy river, Triple Divide peak and Roaring river.

Last week this excursion and others were lived again in reminiscence when Admiral Pond's fellow hikers gathered at Cloyne court at a birthday dinner. The central feature of the occasion was a cake in the form of a huge mountain, decorated with seventy red, white and blue candles and repleted with rock candy and a forest of evergreen twigs. The out-of-doors spirit was heightened when the candles set the toy trees ablaze, giving what the Admiral termed "a first-class forest fire effect."

The birthday party was also featured by an account of the adventure in which the navy man and ...nt Morse, Coast and Geodetic Survey officer, were the central figures many years ago. The story recalled the naming of Mt. Tired, Alaska, when the Admiral and Morse, in 1882, climbed the peak and were forced to spend the night in the open, returning to their ship the following day in the physical condition which resulted in the jocular naming of "Tired, Mountain."

The Admiral regards his advancing years but lightly, and his conversation gives no hint of his ever abandoning his favorite pastime.

Rear-Admiral Charles F. Pond, retired

Women Vote for President

and for all other officers in all elections on the same terms as men in

Wyoming, Colorado, Utah and Idaho

Why Not in California?

ADDRESS

Mrs. J. V. McBean
El Monte Av.
R.D. Mt. View
California

PALO ALTO CAL. 7-AM 1909

Post Card

VOTE YES

Senate Amendment No. 8

OCT. 10 · 1911

JUSTICE FOR CALIFORNIA WOMEN

Give your girl an equal chance with your boy.

THESE STATES HAVE EQUAL SUFFRAGE
Wyoming. Colorado. Idaho. Utah. Washington.

CALIFORNIA NEXT!

An attack on Woman Suffrage is an attack on democracy.
College Equal Suffrage League.

4TH PLACE ON BALLOT

*Berkeley, California*
*May–November 1896*

To Beth, Lynn, Mary, Mary, and Meghan.
Thank you for marching with me.
—C. R. M.

For Lesly, idea person and determined
under-the-radar rebel, with love and thanks.
—S. S.

Thanks to the archive staff of the Bancroft Library at the University of California for their assistance in examining the Keith-McHenry-Pond Family papers, and to Mary Virginia Culbertson, Bessie's niece and Charlie's daughter, who graciously told me about her family history. Writer-illustrator Teri Sloat accompanied me on a research trip to the Bancroft archives and responded to many versions of this story. My Spokane writing group—Lynn Caruso, Beth Cooley, Mary Douthitt, Mary Cronk Farrell, and Meghan Nuttall Sayres—offered detailed feedback. An early version was read at a residency of the Hamline MFAC, a vibrant community of faculty and student writers. Finally, thanks to my husband and my ninety-two-year-old mother, who never stopped believing in me, and to Conor, Megan, and my extended family, who keep listening to my stories.

Published by
PEACHTREE PUBLISHERS
1700 Chattahoochee Avenue
Atlanta, Georgia 30318-2112
*www.peachtree-online.com*



Illustrations rendered in gouache on
Fabriano Artistico watercolor paper

Printed in April 2015 by Imago in Singapore
10 9 8 7 6 5 4 3

Library of Congress Cataloging-in-Publication Data

Murphy, Claire Rudolf.
Marching with Aunt Susan: Susan B. Anthony and the fight for women's suffrage / written by Claire Rudolf Murphy ; illustrated by Stacey Schuett.
p. cm.
Summary: Not allowed to go hiking with her father and brothers because she is a girl, Bessie learns about women's rights when she attends a suffrage rally led by Susan B. Anthony.
ISBN 978-1-56145-593-5
[1. Sex role--Fiction. 2. Women's rights--Fiction. 3. Women--Suffrage--Fiction. 4. Anthony, Susan B. (Susan Brownell), 1820-1906--Fiction.] I. Schuett, Stacey, ill. II. Title.
PZ7.M9525Mar 2011
[E]--dc22

2011002703

# MARCHING WITH AUNT SUSAN

## Susan B. Anthony and the Fight for Women's Suffrage

Written by Claire Rudolf Murphy

Illustrated by Stacey Schuett

PEACHTREE
ATLANTA

Papa took my brothers hiking, but not me.

"Strenuous exercise is not for girls, Bessie," he told me.

"You're not strong enough," Enie said.

"It's not ladylike," Charlie added.

"I can ride my bicycle faster than anyone on the block," I told my brothers. "Even you."

"Girls shouldn't ride bicycles either," Charlie said.

And they left without me.

Inside, Mama bustled around, preparing for a party.

"I'm strong enough to hike," I said. "Papa wouldn't take me along, just because I'm a girl."

"You can help me get ready for the suffrage tea," Mama said. "Aunt Mary will be arriving soon with our guest of honor, Miss Susan B. Anthony."

"Suffrage? I'm the one who's suffering." I picked up the newspaper and stared at Miss Anthony's photo. "She looks like a crabby old lady."

"A crabby old lady who has fought fifty years for women's rights," Mama said, "even when people threw garbage at her and called her names."

At the tea, everybody swarmed around Miss Anthony. They called her Aunt Susan, even though they weren't related to her.

She spoke about the long fight for equal rights. She told us that children should grow up in a world where both men and women were free.

Later, Aunt Mary introduced me to Aunt Susan.

"Why can't girls do the same things as boys?" I asked her.

She shook her head. "When I was your age, my teacher thought only boys were smart enough to learn long division."

"That's not right," I said.

"Come to the rally in San Francisco tomorrow, Bessie. Women's votes can help change the world."

Golden Gate Auditorium was so crowded that I could barely breathe. Aunt Susan stood on a stage, surrounded by hundreds of roses. Her voice thundered across the hall. "The votes of all the people, including women with men, will surely bring about the wisest and best government the world has ever seen."

I pulled a white handkerchief out of my purse and joined the sea of flags waving in the air.

The day after the rally, I rode my bicycle over to my best friend Rita's house. "You should have heard Aunt Susan speak yesterday," I told her.

"My papa says ladies shouldn't speak in public," Rita said.

"Aunt Susan says that girls are just as smart as boys. We should get to help make decisions too."

"Papa decides everything in our family," Rita said.

"That's not right." I looked at my best friend. "Someday I want to vote. Let's see if we can help out at suffrage headquarters."

All through the summer, Rita and I wrote letters, licked envelopes, and painted posters. As we worked, we listened to women talk.

*"Men decide everything. They even decide*
*if we should get to vote."*
*"Men decide how the children are raised."*
*"Men decide how the household money is spent."*

"I don't understand," I said to Rita. "I get to spend my allowance any way I want. And Mama makes decisions about lots of our purchases."

"Not at our house." Rita shook her head. "Papa keeps track of every penny."

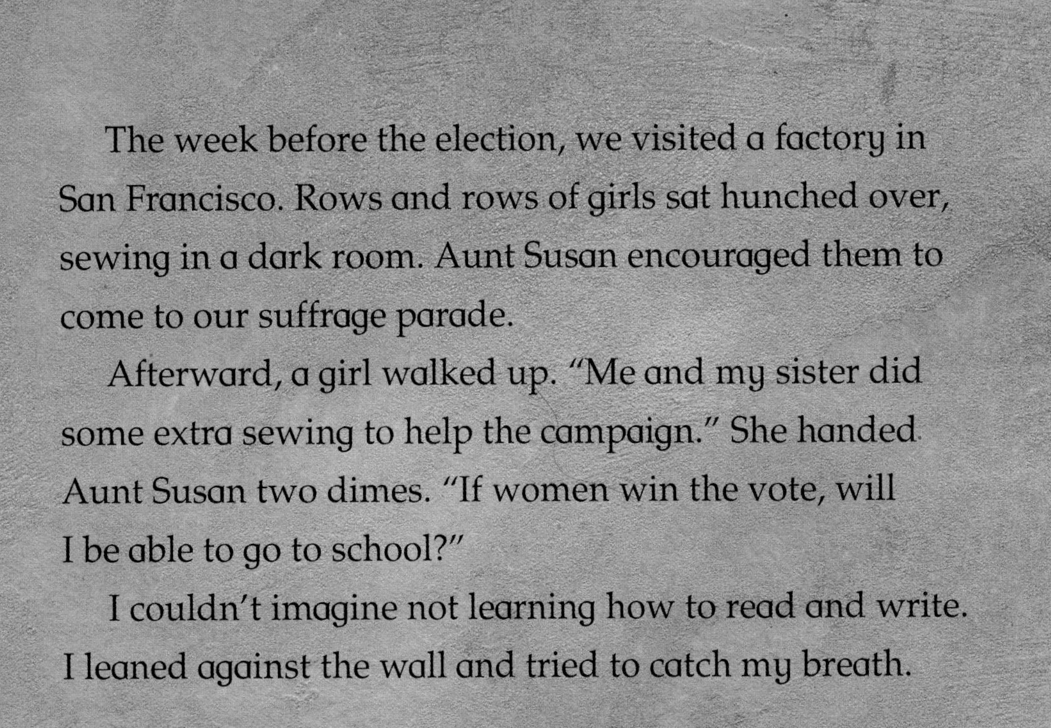

The week before the election, we visited a factory in San Francisco. Rows and rows of girls sat hunched over, sewing in a dark room. Aunt Susan encouraged them to come to our suffrage parade.

Afterward, a girl walked up. "Me and my sister did some extra sewing to help the campaign." She handed Aunt Susan two dimes. "If women win the vote, will I be able to go to school?"

I couldn't imagine not learning how to read and write. I leaned against the wall and tried to catch my breath.

Back at headquarters, I asked Aunt Susan why those girls didn't go to school.

"Many parents can't make enough money to feed their families," she told me. "So the children have to work."

"Can women getting the vote change that?" I asked.

Aunt Susan nodded. "We can work to pass laws that will help adults *and* children."

I dumped out all the coins in my purse and handed them to her. "If those girls can give money, I should too."

Later I painted a picture of the factory girl on a banner for the parade. Rita printed the letters.

Sunday afternoon before the vote, Rita, Mama, and I marched along, carrying our banner. The crowd cheered as we sang new lyrics to "My Country, 'Tis of Thee."

*Our country, now from thee,*
*Claim we our liberty,*
*In freedom's name.*
*Guarding home's altar fires,*
*Daughters of patriot sires,*
*Their zeal our own inspires,*
*Justice to claim.*

VOTES FOR
SCHOOL FOR
GIRLS AN

But then men began shouting. “Women belong in the kitchen! Girls belong at home!”

Rita’s father appeared and dragged her away. “No daughter of mine will parade in the streets!”

A boy splattered an egg down the front of my white dress. “What do you want to be—a man?” he yelled.

I stood frozen, watching the oozing yellow stain spread, until Mama picked up Rita’s end of the banner and we marched on.

When he heard what had happened, Papa bought me a new white dress. If only it was that easy to win the election.

Monday after school, Mama and I stood at the ferry launch and held up a new sign.

**REMEMBER YOUR DAUGHTERS—VOTE**
**YES on REFERENDUM #6**

I couldn't tell if I got more pats on the head or grumbles from the men walking by. But Mama said, "It only matters how they vote tomorrow."

The day after the election, my brothers raced me home from school. Charlie grabbed the newspaper off the front porch.

"Women Lose the Vote!" he shouted.

I leaned my bicycle against the house and snatched the newspaper out of his hand.

"What are you so mad about?" asked Enie.

"Someday you'll get to vote and you don't even care. Mama is as smart as Papa, and I'm as smart as you. We should get to vote too."

Mama came out and picked up my bicycle. "Aunt Susan says that a bicycle gives a woman freedom. Teach me how to ride, Bessie."

"It's hard to do," I said, sitting down on the steps.

"When you first tried to ride, you kept falling and scraping your knees," she reminded me. "But you didn't give up."

Finally I showed her what to do—how to mount the bicycle, balance, pedal, and drag her feet to stop.

When Papa arrived home, Mama was wobbling up and down the street. "I'm sorry about the election, Bessie," he said.

"Girls should be allowed to do the same things as boys, Papa."

"Why don't we go hiking this Saturday?" he asked.

"Thanks, Papa," I said, grabbing his hand. "And Sunday there's a rally for the next suffrage campaign. Come march with Mama and me."

## AUTHOR'S NOTE

Ever since I learned that women first won the vote in the Western states, I have been fascinated with the seventy-two-year struggle for American women's suffrage. I realized that I had never read about women's suffrage in my college history courses, so I set out to learn all I could. I wanted to find a real girl to write about, and eventually I found the Keith-McHenry-Pond Family Papers at The Bancroft Library at the University of California, Berkeley. Inside boxes and cartons were Bessie's journals, newspaper articles about her family's hiking, and the suffrage collection of her aunt, Mary McHenry Keith. My hands shook as I read letters from my hero Susan B. Anthony to Aunt Mary.

*Marching with Aunt Susan* is based on actual events in the 1896 campaign. The quote from Susan B. Anthony's speech at Golden Gate Auditorium was one she often used. The version of "My Country, 'Tis of Thee" that Bessie sings in the parade was written by Elizabeth Harnett and performed at suffrage meetings around the country.

This story is my chance to march with Aunt Susan and to thank her, Bessie, Aunt Mary, and the hundreds of thousands of women who won the vote for me and for you.

## BESSIE

Bessie Keith Pond was a real girl who lived in Berkeley, California, in 1896. She had two older brothers, Enie (Enoch) and Charlie. Her father Charles was a naval commander. Her mother Emma was a painter and poet, who invented the board game Constitution. Bessie grew up in a family of avid suffragists: her grandmother, mother, and especially her aunt, Mary McHenry Keith, who was a leader in both California campaigns.

Aunt Mary was the first California woman to graduate from law school and the wife of the well-known landscape painter William Keith. She became close friends with Susan B. Anthony during her 1895 and 1896 trips to California. In 1905, when Anthony returned for one last trip to California, Uncle Willie painted her portrait.

# KEITH POND

(1886–1955)

Bessie wrote poetry and taught art and music all her life. For many years, Bessie, her father, and her brothers took month-long mountain hikes and snowshoe trips in the Sierra Nevada mountains, sometimes up to 300 miles. This was so unusual that the family was often featured in the newspaper. An article in the June 24, 1927, edition of the *San Francisco Call* described Bessie as an "athletic girl with a fondness for outdoor life."

## CALIFORNIA SUFFRAGE CAMPAIGN

In 1895, the California legislature agreed to let men vote on an amendment to the state constitution in support of women's suffrage. That year Susan B. Anthony traveled to California to help get the referendum on the ballot and returned in May 1896 to lead the campaign for the November election.

Hundreds of suffragists across the state organized meetings in every town. Anthony spoke up to thirty times a day at picnics, schools, factories, military encampments, farmers' markets, church conventions, labor meetings, women and men's clubs, and even poolrooms. Women and girls worked at headquarters around the state, and working women stopped by after work to donate money or take home an armload of circulars to fold and address at night. Rallies and tea parties like the ones in the story took place from May through November, along with dinner parties, including one at the Keith home, which Anthony attended.

Ten days before the election, bar owners became worried that women's suffrage could mean passage of a law ending the sale of liquor. They quickly helped register thousands of men and instructed them to vote no.

The final tally was 247,454 votes: 110,355 for; 137,099 against.

The next morning Anthony said, "I don't care for myself. I am used to defeat, but these dear California women who have worked hard, how can they bear it?"

For many years, the suffrage movement languished in California and across America. In 1911, suffragists finally got a referendum back on the California ballot. Young suffragists campaigned in the newly invented automobile and used the telephone to reach voters. On October 10, 1911, fifteen years after the events depicted in this book, California became the sixth and largest state to approve women's suffrage.

# *Susan B. Anthony*

(1820–1906)

Susan B. Anthony was raised as a Quaker with the belief that men and women are equal. But all around her she witnessed inequality. Girls who worked at her father's mill couldn't attend school because their families needed their wages. She and the other girls at her school weren't allowed to learn long division. Later when she became a teacher, she earned only one-quarter the salary of male teachers. All these experiences made her want to work for change.

When Anthony was eighteen years old, she joined the abolitionist movement after hearing Lucretia Mott speak out against slavery. In 1851, she met Elizabeth Cady Stanton and became devoted to the cause of women's suffrage. Anthony believed that if women could vote, they could help pass laws to end slavery and to improve working conditions and the lives of the poor.

For more than fifty years Susan B. Anthony led the fight for women's suffrage along with her friend Elizabeth Cady Stanton. While Stanton wrote speeches and raised a family, Anthony campaigned across the country. She first visited California in 1871 and returned several times, including eight months during the campaign depicted in this book.

Even in her later years, Anthony was described as tireless, working night and day. At a celebration of her eighty-sixth birthday at the 1906 meeting of the National American Women's Suffrage Association, Susan proclaimed her famous rallying cry, "Failure is impossible."

In 1896, one woman reporter said she didn't believe in suffrage—until she interviewed Anthony.

"I WISH I WERE SUSAN B. ANTHONY," SHE WROTE. THERE IS SOMETHING LOVEABLE IN HER FACE AND VOICE. SHE IS BEAUTIFUL IN HER PLAINNESS AND HER SMILE IS NOT TO BE FORGOTTEN."

Susan B. Anthony died in Rochester on March 13, 1906. Memorial services were held all over the country, including one in San Francisco, during which William Keith's portrait of her was unveiled.

After Anthony's death, Bessie's aunt, Mary McHenry Keith, and many other supporters around the country lobbied to make her birthday a national holiday. That never happened. But a dollar coin features her likeness.

Susan B. Anthony died before all American women won the vote in 1920, one hundred years after her birth. But her name is forever linked with the long battle for women's suffrage.

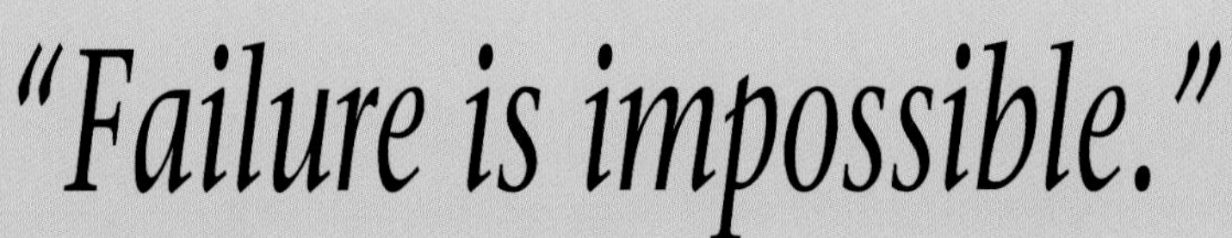

# Suffrage History

Our Constitution states that citizens should be allowed to vote, but it doesn't spell out who is considered to be a citizen. That was left up to each state to decide. In the early days of our country, only male landowners were allowed to vote. Men of color won the right to vote with passage of the Fifteenth Amendment in 1870, but women still could not vote.

Beginning with the first suffrage convention in Seneca Falls, New York, in 1848, women in every state worked to get the vote. The seventy-two-year campaign stretched through two wars and sixteen presidents. It included 56 state referendum campaigns, 480 campaigns to get legislatures to consider suffrage amendments, 47 campaigns for constitutional conventions, 277 campaigns directed at state party conventions, and 30 campaigns to get national parties to put suffrage in their platforms.

In 1878, the Susan B. Anthony amendment was first introduced in Congress. But it wasn't until 1919 that it finally passed both houses of Congress. In August 1920, Tennessee became the thirty-sixth state to ratify the Nineteenth Amendment. One hundred years after Susan B. Anthony's birth, women from every state finally gained the vote.

|  |  |
|---|---|
| 1787 | U.S. Constitution leaves voting rights up to the states to decide. Only New Jersey allows women to vote, and only between 1776 and 1807. |
| 866 | Elizabeth Cady Stanton and Susan B. Anthony form the American Equal Rights Association, an organization for white and black women and men dedicated to the goal of universal suffrage. |
| 869 | Wyoming Territorial legislature grants full voting rights to women. |
| 1870 | Utah Territorial legislature grants full voting rights to women. |
| 1870 | The Fifteenth Amendment allows men of color to vote, but not women. |
| 1872 | Susan B. Anthony attempts to vote in the presidential election and is arrested. |
| 1883 | Washington Territorial legislature grants full voting rights to women. |
| 1890 | Wyoming is the first state to grant full voting rights to women. |
| 1893 | Colorado state referendum grants full voting rights to women. |
| 1896 | Utah and Idaho grant full voting rights to women. Suffrage referendum defeated in California. |
| 1906 | Susan B. Anthony dies. |
| 1910 | Washington state referendum grants full voting rights to women. |
| 1911 | California state referendum grants full voting rights to women. |
| 1912 | Oregon, Kansas, and Arizona grant full voting rights to women. |
| 1913 | Alaska Territorial Legislature grants full voting rights to women. |
| 1914 | Montana and Nevada grant full voting rights to women. |
| 1918 | South Dakota and Oklahoma referenda grant full voting rights to women. |
| 1919 | U.S. House of Representatives and Senate approve the Nineteenth Amendment granting all American women full voting rights. |
| 1920 | The Nineteenth Amendment wins the necessary two-thirds ratification from state legislatures. |

## THE NINETEENTH AMENDMENT TO THE UNITED STATES CONSTITUTION

THE RIGHT OF CITIZENS OF THE UNITED STATES TO VOTE SHALL NOT BE DENIED OR ABRIDGED BY THE UNITED STATES OR BY ANY STATE ON ACCOUNT OF SEX.

CONGRESS SHALL HAVE POWER TO ENFORCE THIS ARTICLE BY APPROPRIATE LEGISLATION.

*"Yes, I'll tell you what I think of bicycling. I think it has done more to emancipate women than any one thing in the world. I rejoice every time I see a woman ride by on a wheel. It gives her a feeling of freedom and self-reliance."*
*—Susan B. Anthony (1896)*

# FURTHER RESOURCES

## FOR YOUNG READERS:

*Failure Is Impossible: Susan B. Anthony in Her Own Words*
written by Lynn Sherr (Times Books)

*The History of Woman Suffrage*, Volume I
edited by Susan B. Anthony and Ida Husted Harper (General Boo

*If You Lived When Women Won Their Rights*
written by Anne Kamma (Scholastic)

*Life and Work of Susan B. Anthony*
written by Ida Husted Harper (Qontro)

*One Woman, One Vote: Rediscovering the Woman Suffrage Movement*
edited by Marjorie Spruill Wheeler (NewSage)

*With Courage and Cloth: Winning the Fight for a Woman's Right to Vote*
written by Ann Bausum (National Geographic)

**Women of the West online exhibit:**
www.theautry.org/explore/exhibits/suffrage/suffrage_ca.html

**National Women's History Museum online exhibit:**
www.nwhm.org/online-exhibits/votesforwomen/suffragetimeline.html

**HerStory:** www.herstoryscrapbook.com
This website features articles, letters, and editorials regarding the suffrage campaign from the *New York Times*

SUSAN B. ANTHONY

*"It's up to you, Mary, and all your marvelous friends."*

*—Susan B. Anthony*

*in a letter to Bessie's aunt*

Credits for the materials reproduced on the endpapers:

"Mariner, 76, Still Spry After 360 Mile Hike Up Coast With Daughter," *Oakland Tribune*, August 2, 1927, courtesy of The Bancroft Library, University of California, Berkeley, Keith-McHenry-Pond Family Papers

"Suffrage march line—How thousands of women parade today at Capital" graphic, courtesy of the Library of Congress

Cover of *The Anthony Home Calendar*, courtesy of the Library of Congress

"When a Fellow Needs a Friend" cartoon by Briggs from the *New York Tribune,* courtesy of The Bancroft Library, University of California, Berkeley, Keith-McHenry-Pond Family Papers

"Votes for Women" cartoon, courtesy of the Library of Congress

Photograph of suffragists, courtesy of California State Library (4427-b)

"Pond to Command Pacific Reserve Fleet," *San Francisco Chronicle,* April 14, 1915, courtesy of The Bancroft Library, University of California, Berkeley, Keith-McHenry-Pond Family Papers

Front page of the *Woman's Journal and Suffrage News,* courtesy of the Library of Congress

"Women Vote for President" postcard, courtesy of The Bancroft Library, University of California, Berkeley, Keith-McHenry-Pond Family Papers

"Veteran Navy Officer Takes Delight in Trips to High California Mountain Tops," *San Francisco Chronicle*, November 14, 1926, courtesy of The Bancroft Library, University of California, Berkeley, Keith-McHenry-Pond Family Papers

"Vote Yes" poster, courtesy of Huntington Library/SBA/CA/Clippings (1) #49

"Election Day!" cartoon, courtesy of the Library of Congress

Credits for the materials reproduced in the back matter:

Page 32, photograph of Bessie Keith, courtesy of The Bancroft Library, University of California, Berkeley, Keith-McHenry-Pond Family Papers

Page 34, photograph of Susan B. Anthony, courtesy of the Library of Congress

Page 35, photograph of suffragists, courtesy of the Library of Congress

Page 36, photograph of suffragists marching, courtesy of the Library of Congress

Page 36, photograph of suffragist holding "Failure Is Impossible" banner, courtesy of the Library of Congress

Oakland Tribune

# Mariner, 76, Still Spry After 360 Mile Hike Up Coast With Daughter

Oakland Tribune Aug. 2, 1927

BERKELEY, Aug. 2.—After hiking 360 miles in five weeks, Rear Admiral Charles F. Pond, 76, is back in Berkeley today, feeling no ill effects from his little jaunt and already planning what new section of California he will explore next summer.

"Just a pleasant little hike—that's all," Admiral Pond said today, stepping off at a quick gait on the porch of his home, 2621 Ridge road, to show that his legs are still limber.

The elderly mariner and his daughter, Miss Elizabeth Pond, set off from San Francisco five weeks ago on their annual hiking tour, a custom they have followed since Admiral Pond's retirement from active service nine years ago. They followed the tortuous California shore line as closely as possible, working their way down the coast along spray-swept beaches and over cliffs and cattle trails.

"We made from seven to 18 miles every day," chuckled the admiral. "We were on a pleasure hike, and didn't attempt to set any speed records."

"How did you manage about sleeping and eating?" he was asked.

**BOTH KEPT WARM**

"That was simple," was the immediate reply. "We slept wherever we felt like it, and ate whenever we were hungry. We carried our own bedding, food, and cooking utensils, and camped wherever we found a likely spot. At night we rolled up in our blankets underneath the stars. No, we weren't cold. I've rigged up a pretty good protection against that. I wore an aviator's helmet—sort of an out-of-door nightcap, you might say. My daughter tied a silk handkerchief around her head, and we kept warm and comfortable."

Upon reaching Pismo Beach, their objective, Admiral Pond and his daughter took an auto stage, making the return trip to Berkeley in one day. The couple make a pilgrimage to some little-traveled portion of the state every year, due to an incurable habit formed by the old sea-warrior during the regime of Roosevelt.

"We had to walk in those days," said the admiral, a twinkle in his eyes. "I've never gotten over it."

**FARMERS IMPRESS**

The couple were particularly impressed on this hike with the character of the farmers they met along the sea coast. Most of them, says Admiral Pond, are typical "close-to-the-soil" Americans, old settlers who have lived with the trade winds blowing in off the Pacific [illegible] all their lives. The[illegible] [illegible] and wonderfully [illegible] to the occasional [illegible] who wanders off the beat[illegible] to their doors, he avers.

Three years ago the adm[illegible] his daughter traversed the northern section of the California coast, making their way from Sausalito to Eureka. They have cover[illegible] Yosemite hinterland thorou[illegible] have climbed Mt. Whitney, an[illegible] familiar with nearly all the sno[illegible] capped passes of the high S[illegible]

"EQUAL RIGHTS FOR ALL."

# The Anthony Home Calendar

WITH SELECTIONS FROM THE LETTERS AND SPEECHES OF MISS ANTHONY. ILLUSTRATED BY FRANCES B. JOHNSTON. COPYRIGHT, 1900, BY CATHARINE M. FLEMING.

REAR-ADMIRAL Charles F. Pond, who will succeed to command of Pacific reserve fleet on May 5th. Chronicle April 14, 1915

FRASER PHOTO

# POND TO COMMAND PACIFIC RESERVE FLEET

## To Succeed Rear-Admiral Doyle, Who Will Be Retired for Age on May 5th.

WASHINGTON, April 13.—Secretary Daniels today designated Rear-Admiral Charles F. Pond, now superintendent of the Twelfth Naval district, with headquarters at Mare Island, to succeed Rear-Admiral Robert M. Doyle as commander-in-chief of the Pacific reserve fleet. Rear-Admiral Doyle will be retired for age on May 5th next. Admiral Pond's successor has not yet been selected.

*How Thousands of Women Parade To-day at Capital.*

# SUFFRAGE MARCH LINE

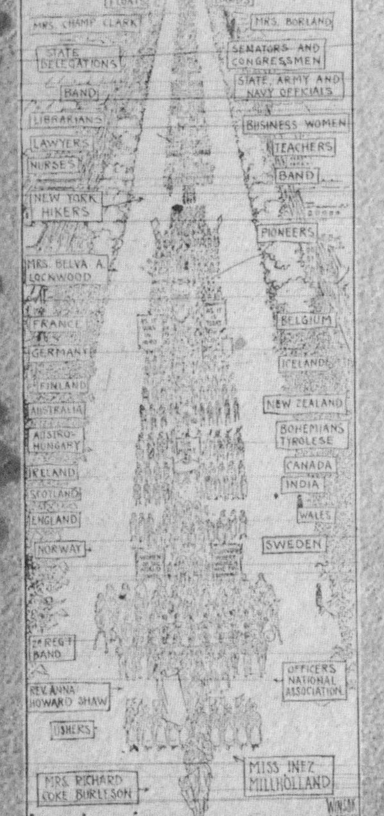

"When a Fellow Needs a Friend"

Courtesy of New York Tribune.